About the Author

Milovan Glišić (1847 – 1908) was a gifted and highly prolific 19th century Serbian translator, author, dramaturg, and writer. His literary works tended towards social and political satire, criticizing corruption, exploitation of peasants, the effects of modernization, and bureaucracy. His best-known works include *Short Stories* and the plays *Hoax* and *Two Farthings*. In addition to translating the major Russian authors of his day – among them Gogol, Pushkin, Turgenev, Tolstoy, Chekhov, Dostoevsky, and Gorky -- he also translated Balzac and Verne from French, and Twain and Poe from English.

D1521062

About the Translator

James Lyon holds a Ph.D. in Balkan History from UCLA, is founder of the Foundation for the Preservation of Historical Heritage, and an Associate Researcher with the Zentrum für Südosteuropastudien at the University of Graz. He has spent over three decades studying and working with the lands of the former Yugoslavia. He is author of the vampire-themed novel *Kiss of the Butterfly*, which is set in the Balkans amidst the breakup of Yugoslavia, and *Serbia and the Balkan Front, 1914: the Outbreak of the Great War*.

After Ninety Years

MILOVAN GLIŠIĆ

translated by

James Lyon

Contents

Pronunciation Guide

Sava Savanović...Sah-vah Sah-van-o-vich

Zarožje...Za-rozh-ye

Ovčina...Ov-chee-na

Živan Dušman...Zhi-van Duush-man

Raško Ćebo..Rash-ko Che-bo

Strahinja...Strakh-in-ya

Radojka...Radojka

Purko..Pur-ko

Mirko..Meer-ko

Đilas..Jee-lass

Srećko...Sretch-ko

Srdan...Sir-dan

Zarožani...Za-rozh-ani

Ovčani..Ohv-chani

Mirjana...Meer-yah-na

Mirjanić..Meer-yah-nich

Translator's Note

The vampire as we know it today is a creature that is rooted firmly in pan-Slavic pagan cosmology. As such, substantial similarities in vampire mythology and legend exist among all the Slavic peoples. Because Christianity succeeded in largely erasing the Slavic pagan traditions, far less is known of the pagan Slavic mythology and cosmology than of comparable Egyptian, Norse, Roman, or Greek beliefs.

Vampires have a rich and well-documented history in the Balkans, dating back at least to Article 20 of Serbian Tsar Stefan Dušan's 1349 Law Code, which forbade the exhumation and killing of corpses by "witchcraft". The first recorded use of the word "vampire" (*vampyri*) in history came from Serbia (not Romania) in 1725, the famous case of Peter Plogojowitz in the village of Kisiljevo. During 1731, the Austrian Army sent a regimental surgeon, Johann Flückinger, to conduct a series of exhumations and autopsies of suspected vampires in Serbia, the results of which he documented and subsequently published as *Visum et Repertum* (Leipzig, 1732), a work that is widely credited with introducing the word "vampire" into use in other languages.

The Balkans gave us other vampire-related historical incidents. In 1403, the Croatian coastal city of Zadar had a well-documented case of a vampire from the nearby island of Pašman, Priba, who was exhumed and staked by order of the city council. The Vojvoda of Wallachia, Vlad III, Tsepeș, also known as Dracula, visited the Bosnian town of Srebrenica in 1476 and conducted a bloody massacre there. In 1666, in the Adriatic coastal town of Ston, a man named Stjepan Nikolin offered his services as a vampire slayer, while in 1672 the Croatian town of Kringa (Kranjska) was terrorized by a vampire, Djura Grando. From 1736 to 1744, the Dubrovnik Court put twelve men on trial for digging up graves of suspected vampires. In 1833, Ottoman Turkish authorities in the Bulgarian town of Tirnovo were confronted with a case of two former Janissaries who had become vampires, which required them to engage a Christian specialist to stake the suspected corpses. These, of course, are but a few examples of vampire-related activities in the Balkans.

Given this cultural context, it should come as no surprise that the well-known 19th century Serbian author, Milovan Glišić, would write a story about a vampire, in this case, the legendary 18th century vampire Sava Savanović from the village of Zarožje. Because Glišić wrote before Bram Stoker's *Dracula* introduced bats and Transylvania to the vampire trope, he based his story on the folktales and folk beliefs of villagers.

After Ninety Years was part of a collection entitled *Short Stories* (*Pripovetke*). The language Glišić employs is the vernacular of the uneducated and illiterate rural population in the mountainous regions of western Serbia along the Drina River valley in the 18th and 19th centuries. In contrast to the heavily ornamented and wordy prose so common among his 19th century contemporaries in Russia and the west, Glišić deliberately wrote in a sparse, plain, and raw style, accurately reflecting the mannerisms of village life and culture, an approach used by Mark Twain in *The Celebrated Jumping Frog of Calaveras County*. I have attempted to maintain this sense of rawness in the translation.

To emphasize the coarse character of village speech, Glišić makes rather liberal use of exclamation marks and ellipses. For the sake of clarity and readability, I was forced to remove many of these punctuation marks. I chose, however, to retain Glišić's use of dashes. Thus, the structure of the text is a faithful visual replication of the actual appearance in Serbian.

Similar to 19th century American author Washington Irving's *The Legend of Sleepy Hollow* or *Rip Van Winkle*, Glišić mined local folklore to retell the story of the vampire Sava Savanović. As such, the text presents a wealth of ethnographic material. How faithfully Glišić actually adhered to the original story is unclear, as I encountered variations of the Sava Savanović legend in and around Zarožje, where the story is set. These differ mainly in regard to Savanović's background and the interaction between the protagonist Strahinja and the father of his intended.

For the careful observer, Glišić offers valuable insights into the roles of women and children in the traditional patriarchal Serbian *zadruga*, a family-based agricultural cooperative that formed the basis of village life. The role of alcohol in hospitality, causing and settling disputes is also quite evident. And village gossip plays an important role in the everyday life of both men and women. Of particular note is Glišić's description of the folk beliefs surrounding vampires, how they are found, how they are killed, the forms they take, their physical appearance, etc. In this, Glišić accurately reflects folk beliefs still present today in many rural areas of the Balkans.

Glišić's villagers speak extensively using the aorist tense, a phenomenon quite common even today in rural and isolated parts of the Balkans. They also use many words and expression that have since disappeared from widespread use. This presents difficulties both for modern native speakers of Serbo-Croatian and translators alike. Even today, many college-educated urban Serbs have difficulty understanding some of the expressions, and many of the words are found only in highly specialized dictionaries, or in some cases, not at all.

Thus, a modern Serb will experience many of the same difficulties understanding *After Ninety Years* as would a modern English speaker when reading Scottish author Sir Walter Scott's highland adventure novels *Rob Roy* or *Waverly* (1814, 1817). Similar to Scott, Glišić uses a vernacular that even then was difficult for many city-dwellers to comprehend. The difficulties in comprehension are compounded by the passage of time, changing cultural references, the impact of modernization, and the standardization of the Serbo-Croatian language.

Yet, the relative lack of urban development in many parts of the Balkans means that there are still many isolated towns and villages both in Serbia and Bosnia where the manner of speech, expressions, and vocabulary used by Glišić remain relatively unchanged. This meant that when dictionaries proved of no avail, I was able to decipher the meaning of some passages by talking with people in isolated rural areas of Serbia and Bosnia, where many of these words remain in use to this day. This included the village of Zarožje itself.

The actual village of Zarožje is not a village in the typical western European sense of the word, with homes clustered around a central green or commercial center. Rather, it consists of isolated homes scattered about the hills and mountain sides of the Zarožje area. This means that there is often little contact among outlying households, and that communication with the outside world is sparse; in 2015, there was no mobile telephone reception in Zarožje. Much of the local agrarian economy is centered on the staples of Balkan mountain life: plums, sheep, garlic, grains, cheese, smoked meat, corn, peppers, onions, cabbage, moonshine (*rakija*), and attendant activities.

During my numerous visits to Zarožje, I was privileged to enjoy the hospitality of the watermill's owner, Slobodan Jagodić, and his wife, who freely shared the bounty of their farm with me – fresh homemade cheeses and *kajmak*, homemade fruit juices, apples, plums, grapes, home baked bread, their own homemade prosciutto (*pršut*), and other delicacies.

When Mr. Jagodić showed me around the watermill, it became evident that Glišić had never actually set eyes on it. Had he done so, his description of it would have been quite different. The watermill – while situated in the bottom of a narrow ravine – is not stuck to a large boulder like a swallow's nest, as Glišić describes it. Likewise, the watermill is quite small and had very little space above the main (and only) room for a loft. This is crucial to Glišić's account, as the protagonist Strahinja lies on his stomach in the loft with his pistols arrayed before him, waiting for the vampire to appear. In reality, the actual watermill is slightly more than four meters in length, making it impossible for events to occur exactly as Glišić described them.

Sadly, the roof of the Zarožje watermill collapsed in the winter of 2012 due to heavy snowfall and rotting timbers. Since then, the mill has been deteriorating gradually, and the interior is open to the elements. On a visit in early October 2015, only one wall remained standing and the floorboards had rotted through, offering a view of the stream below. It does not appear that anyone in the local community has either the resources or desire to repair it.

Any translation is a question of compromise, if for no other reason than the mere fact that language is highly subjective. So too, input from diverse voices is needed to create a coherent and meaningful narrative that is true to the author, the time period, and the spirit of the original work. I am indebted to numerous people for proof-reading the translation. Among them are Dr. Kenneth Morrison (De Montfort University), Dr. Lisa Lampert-Weissig (University of California, San Diego), Dr. Grant Lundberg (Brigham Young University), Andrew Boylan, Anthony Hogg (The Vampirologist), John Furnari, Dr. James K. Lyon (Brigham Young University, emeritus), Therese Nelson, and Jelena Bjelica. I am also indebted to Slobodan Jagodić and his wife, and the facebook group *Pravopis i gramatika srpskog(a) jezika*.

My long-suffering wife, Maja, put up with endless questions at inconvenient hours regarding the syntax, meaning, and expressions of her native language. She then went on to design the terrific book jacket. My mother-in-law provided carbohydrates with plates of homemade warm *gibanice*, *palačinke*, and *pita*. If the text is of use, it is due entirely to the efforts of these good people. Any mistakes are entirely my own.

James Lyon
Belgrade, October 2015.

MILOVAN GLIŠIĆ

Foreword

There are many great Nineteenth Century vampire stories, some more obscure than others. One of the joys of that era of vampire literature was the experimentation. Until Bram Stoker published *Dracula* at the end of the century (1897), there was much less of a commonality in the lore used, and as such, many of the works seem much more inventive to our modern eyes.

The vampire was an often-used subject, but it has only been recently that some of the Nineteenth Century works have been translated to allow access to English speaking students of vampire lore, most notably the rich *oeuvre* of French vampire stories. What, however, of Slavic vampire stories? After all, the word "vampire" was introduced to the English speaking world from Serbia when the March 11, 1732 edition of the *London Journal* used the word in association with the Arnont Paule case. (Hogg, 2009)

The novel the *Pobratim: A Slav Novel* was released in English by Prof. P. Jones in 1895 and contains a variety of Slavic folktales, amongst which we hear of vampires. However Milovan Glišić's 1880 vampire story *Posle Devedeset Godina* has not, to my knowledge, ever been translated into English before. Being that Glišić was a Serbian, I have always hoped that it would be a rich and full story. Indeed I was potentially familiar with the story as it had been filmed, in 1973, by Đorđe Kadijević as *Leptirica* or the she-butterfly – a fitting title for, as we will discuss, the butterfly or moth was a very important element of Serbian vampire myth. Of course films and books notoriously part company when it comes to plot.

When I gained the opportunity to look over an early draft of this translation I was, suffice it to say, filled with excitement and I wasn't disappointed. Whilst the film added a large coda to the story that the original prose did not contain, which substantially changes the story's outcome, I could see that Kadijević had stuck closely to the original text to a point; though even then there were textual details that were altered. For instance, in the text the overbearing father Živan is opposed to the relationship between his daughter, Radojka, and the story's hero Strahinja. This is partly because he sees the (actually industrious) young man as a wastrel, but no further reasoning is offered, and Živan actually seems opposed to any suitor. In the film Strahinja is deemed as too poor, but Živan is actively seeking suitors for the girl. Likewise Strahinja is talked into becoming a reluctant miller in the film, whereas, in the prose, he actively volunteers to be the miller and can't be dissuaded. But why does he become a miller?

The watermill is a primary part of the story and was lifted from the actual folklore surrounding Sava Savanović, who is the vampire of the story. In folklore Savanović was said to haunt a watermill on the Rogačica River that, until 2012, was still an extant structure called Jagodića Vodenica. In 2012 the watermill collapsed leading to a tongue-in-cheek health warning being released by the local authorities, suggesting that Savanović would be looking for a new home – though some Western reports of the warning took the announcement somewhat more seriously. (Nelson, 2012) In both the prose and the film we discover that the millers who have worked in the mill at night have all died. The prose suggests that death was by strangulation, whereas the film has Savanović bite the millers, and the attack of a miller becomes the opening of the film. It should be noted that the location fits well within Slavic myth, as John V. A. Fine Jr cites 19th century Serbian writer and ethnographer Vuk Karadžić as saying, "in times of hunger vampires often gather near mills and around granaries." (Fine Jr, 1998, p. 58)

Strahinja's activity in the mill differs between the prose and the film. In the film his activity is clumsy, his survival accidental and – once he manages to cover himself in flour – he is assumed to be some form of spectre when the village men arrive in the morning. In the prose he is deliberate and brave, shooting the vampire with pistols loaded with both steel and Turkish coins called *marjaš*. There is, one feels, significance to the coins – though when the vampire is discovered later he is already recovering from the gunshot wounds. Strahinja tricks the vampire by hiding logs beneath a blanket and, in so doing, hears the vampire's name – allowing the villagers to eventually discover where the vampire is buried. The vampire himself looks very different in the two mediums. In the prose he is (sparingly) described as a tall man with a face as red as blood, who seems to be able to pass through an unopened door. In the film we see details, rather than the whole face, but he is certainly hirsute and has sharp claws and viciously pointed teeth.

The film and prose both use Živan's stallion to find the unmarked grave of the vampire, the prose being clear that it must be a stallion rather than a gelding. This is again lifted out of Slavic myth and so, returning to John V. A. Fine Jr's citation of Vuk Karadžić, we discover, "they take a black stallion without any spots or marks to the graveyard and lead it among the graves where it is suspected there are *vukodlaks*, for they say that such a stallion does not dare to step over a *vukodlak*." (Fine Jr, 1998, p. 58) In the prose this goes further and the black stallion actually digs at the earth. Whilst relatively uncommon, such lore has found its way into the Western vampire lore, notably in a film version of *Dracula* (1979, director John Badham) where a white horse (rather than black) is used to indicate that Mina[*] has been turned in to a vampire as it paws at the earth of her grave.

In the prose, when the grave of a vampire is found it needs to be opened and the corpse staked with a hawthorn stake (in the prose the coffin is opened, but in the film the stake is hammered through the lid). The film has a priest pray over the grave but the prose suggests

---

[*] In the 1979 production of *Dracula* the roles of Mina and Lucy are reversed.

both prayers and a sprinkling of holy water are needed. There is also a point made in the prose that the vampire hunters must take care not to get the vampire's blood on them – though the narrative does not explain why. However both mediums agree that those at the grave must look for a butterfly emerging from the grave. Friedrich S. Krauss suggests "the others present watch for the appearance of a moth (or butterfly) flying away from the grave. If one does fly out of the grave, everyone runs after it in order to capture it. If it is caught, it is thrown onto a bonfire so that it will die. Only then is the vampire completely destroyed. If the butterfly escapes, however, then, alas, woe to the village…" (Krauss, 1998, p. 68) The butterfly represents the vampire's soul.

The use of moths and butterflies in Western vampire lore is not unknown, but again not overly common. In *Dracula* the vampire is able to control (amongst other creatures) moths (Stoker, 1897, p. 336), and Stoker recognises the fact that a butterfly often represents the soul, generally, when he has Renfield suggest "The ancients did well when they typified the soul as a butterfly!" (Stoker, 1897, p. 373) Though Renfield's words make Seward erroneously suppose that the madman wishes to devour souls. In the *Moth Diaries* (2011, director Mary Harron), the vampire can take the form of a moth (or more precisely moths) it appears, as can the Marvel vampire character Satana, and in the *Blood Beast Terror* (1968, director Vernon Sewell) the vampire is, actually, a large hominid-like moth that suffered the fate of SFX so terrible that not even the inimitable Peter Cushing could save the film. However, the association of moths and/or butterflies specifically with the vampire's soul is a rarity in Western lore, but clearly important within the Slavic myths and perfectly realised in both the prose and the film.

The biggest story difference between prose and film is the end section of the film, which was invented by Kadijević and turns the film towards a much bleaker finale than the original story. This extended ending leads to the film's title being in the feminine. The feel of the two mediums was different also, with the film carrying a dreamlike, almost fairy-tale, quality whereas the prose has a much earthier, folky feel. Kadijević would go on to direct the 1990 film *Sveto Mesto* (*Holy Place*), a dramatization of another great piece of nineteenth century vampire prose, *Viy* by Nikolai Gogol (1835).

For us, however, in the twenty-first century we now, as English speakers, have the opportunity to read a wonderful insight into Slavic vampire myth.

Andrew M. Boylan

Blackpool, UK, 2015

Works Cited

Fine Jr, J. V., 1998. "In Defense of Vampires". In: A. Dundes, ed. *The Vampire A Casebook*. Wisconsin: University of Wisconsin Press, pp. 57-66.

Hogg, A., 2009. *When Did Vampires Enter the English Language?*. [Online]
Available at: http://doaav.blogspot.co.uk/2009/06/when-did-

vampires-enter-english.html
[Accessed 13 August 2015].

Krauss, F. S., 1998. "South Slavic Countermeasures Against Vampires". In: A. Dundes, ed. *The Vampire a Casebook*. Wisconsin: University of Wisconsin Press, pp. 67-71.

Nelson, S. C., 2012. *Vampire Sava Savanovic Is On The Loose, Serbian Village Council Warns (Seriously)*. [Online]
Available at:
http://www.huffingtonpost.co.uk/2012/12/03/vampire-sava-savanovic-serbian-council-warns-_n_2231171.html
[Accessed 13 September 2025].

Stoker, B., 1897. *The New Annotated Dracula*. First (2008) ed. New York: W. W. Norton & Company.

MILOVAN GLIŠIĆ

After Ninety Years

Way back when the *Zarožani*[1] shoved walnuts into the loft with pitchforks; when they watered willow trees and sowed salt;[2] when they went in multitudes into the mountains to cut toothpicks to pick their teeth; when they stretched out boards,[3] dove into kids' wool,[4] carried armloads of hot coals into the house by hand, and so forth…[5] A certain Živan Dušman, the village headman [*Kmet*] in Ovčina, had a remarkably beautiful daughter. Some had already begun to propose to her, but Živan wouldn't even permit betrothal to be mentioned. They say that he even fought with some suitors… Who knows? They might

---

[1] Residents of the village of Zarožje.
[2] Willow trees grow only in marshy and swampy areas and have no need of being watered. Sowing salt renders the soil infertile.
[3] A local joke about people who were too stupid to properly measure boards when building a home, and would then try to stretch out the cut boards when they were too short.
[4] A local joke about people who are so stupid that they jumped from the protruding rocks above Zarožje into the fog below, thinking it was soft kids' wool.
[5] These are all nonsensical acts that portray the people as primitive and stupid.

be lying.

Whatever the case, at some point Živan had begun to snap at his daughter. In truth he shouted at all the children in the house, but he didn't bark at anyone the way he did at her.

One morning, just when she had led the sheep out and was driving them up to pasture, Živan flew out of the house and bellowed:

-'Do you hear me, Radojka?'

-'I hear you, Papa,' she answered slowly, feeling a chill.

-'If I see you once more with the sheep in that copse, don't bother to come home! What are you doing there? Are there not pastures on other hills?'

-'Well… that… there are…' Radojka stammered.

-'Sure there are! But that ragamuffin Strahinja, who frolics on his *frula*[6] all day isn't there! If I get my hands on him I'll skin him!'

Radojka simply lowered her eyes and trembled like a reed.

-'Drive the sheep up to the grove,' Živan hollered, then returned into the house in a nasty mood.

She headed sluggishly uphill with the sheep, towards the glen directly above the house. She turned around often and listened.

The house was in an uproar. Živan raged and shouted, and you would have said he was going to kill everybody. Two children fled outside, bawling.

Radojka herded the sheep a bit quicker, just to distance herself so that she wouldn't hear the uproar. She was a humble and quiet girl,

---

[6] A double shepherd's flute.

lamb-like.

Živan was a frightful man, which is why they called him 'Dušman,' the 'Foe.' He loved to argue with a man more than he loved to drink a glass of *rakija*.[7] And he liked to fight often. Since they had made him *Kmet*, he lost his temper easily.

Radojka had already moved with the sheep beyond the glen and up onto the meadow, so she let them graze down towards the birch grove on the other side of the hill. She sat down on the grass, right there next to the village path, took her knitting out of her bag and began to knit. She had barely turned two or three stitches when Strahinja burst from out of the birch grove below and came to her.

-'Oh, Strahinja, you truly scared me!' Radojka said and turned away bashfully.

-'Is this where you're grazing the sheep?' asked Strahinja, smiling.

-'Leave me alone! Papa will stick me in a cannon!'

-'I know. He won't let you meet with me.'

-'I fear he'll appear from somewhere. He stayed at home. It seems he's beating the children. I fled so I wouldn't have to listen.'

-'A horrible man!' said Strahinja.

-'This morning he wanted to fight with Old Man Sredoje.'

-'Did he come?' asked Strahinja.

-'Who?'

-'Why Old Man Sredoje.'

-'Early this morning. Papa had just washed, then he came.'

---

[7] Home-made moonshine liquor.

-'And?'

-'Well, I don't know what they spoke of… Then Papa shouted something. Old Man Sredoje walked out and said angrily: "What are you blathering about? Just because I mentioned something, it doesn't mean I split your head open." And he left without a word of farewell.'

-'Have you told me truly?' asked Strahinja as though he couldn't believe it.

-'Truly, by God.'

-'I really wish you hadn't told me that,' he said, becoming despondent.

-'Why?' asked Radojka, surprised.

-'Because!' answered Strahinja, and began to ponder.

Just as Radojka started to speak and ask him something, Živan appeared from above on the road and shouted:

-'There you are, *lola*[8]!'

-'Run, Strahinja,' screamed Radojka, and fled towards the sheep on the hillside.

-'Drag yourself home!' Živan bellowed at her and ran towards Strahinja, growling through his teeth: 'Stop, *lola*, stop!'

At first Strahinja was astonished and stood as though rooted. But when he saw that Živan wasn't joking, but was picking up a large rock to throw at him, he fled as fast as he could through the beech grove. Luckily for him, Živan stumbled on some logs and did a nosedive on the heath, or who knows what would have happened.

---

[8] A '*lola*' is a lazy person who likes the good life, wine, women, and food.

In truth, Strahinja was a very courageous and strong lad. He would only grudgingly have backed down from anyone else, but Živan was Radojka's father, so he decided to keep his distance.

By the time Živan arose from the logs there was no sign of Strahinja, nor Radojka, nor the sheep. He then proceeded along the road through the beech grove, grumbling and cursing to himself. He headed into someone's field to assess some damaged crops. It would be difficult for those who did the damage...[9]

Radojka had long ago arrived home with the sheep. Even she herself didn't know where she'd been or how she'd gotten there. At home she found the entire family in fear. She was absolutely dying of fright. Who knew what awaited her when Živan returned.

* * *

Back then in Zarožje, some distance from the village on a stream, in a certain large gorge, there was a country watermill. There the *Zarožani* would grind wheat and eat bread whenever they were hungry. But as if by a miracle of God, they were unable to keep a single miller in that watermill. At dusk he was hale and whole, and at daybreak dead, with a red bruise around his neck as though strangled with a cord. Word of this curiosity spread far, and by now no one dared to be hired as a miller. For several weeks, the *Zarožani* struggled and tinkered with the watermill, grinding a little by day.

---

[9] A village headman acted as a judge. One of his duties was to assess damage to people's crops caused by others. From the context, it is clear that Živan will vent his wrath towards Strahinja against those who spoiled the crops.

And one other thing. At that time there was a *Kmet* in Zarožje, a certain Purko, one of the few *Zarožani* who neither shoved walnuts into the loft with pitchforks, nor drank willow trees, nor stretched boards, nor sowed salt. This Purko was a smart man, even though he wore the longest ponytail in the entire village.

Back then the *Zarožani* didn't cut their hair. Rather, they, and everyone in the surrounding villages wore ponytails. Some down their backs, and some wrapped under their cap behind their necks.

In front of Purko's house was a beautiful meadow; in the meadow a huge spreading walnut tree. Under that walnut tree the people met with the *Kmet* and chatted and agreed about their duties.

Back then there still weren't taverns. Perhaps there were elsewhere, but the *Zarožani* didn't know that taverns existed in the world.[10]

On the feast day of St. John the Baptist,[11] selectmen[12] from the village would sit with the *Kmet* under the walnut tree. Some sat, some lay on their sides, some on their stomachs, and they conversed a bit. The *Kmet* and another two or three men smoked short clay pipes.

The *Kmet* lay on his stomach and kicked his feet slowly: in his hand was some sort of a stick, and he scribbled in the earth in front of him.

-'Alright, people,' began Purko, scribbling a bit in front of him with the branch, 'what shall we do with our watermill? There isn't a miller, nor can we find one. If we at least had two waterwheels it

[10] This is used as an indicator of how primitive life was.
[11] 7 July.
[12] This refers to the village elders, typically the heads of the larger *zadruge*.

would be sufficient to grind by day -- let the devil take the night. But the way things are, we are all suffering without flour. The village is large, there's one water wheel, a backlog... How will it be able to grind for everyone when it grinds only by day?'

-'Even then, brother,' agreed a certain Old Man Mirko, 'a watermill can't be left alone. There's always something that needs to be repaired, the millrace to be cleaned, the millstones dressed... as it is we have more than enough work.'

-'Thank God!' said the *Kmet* and kicked his legs a little. 'Everything is good in the village. The sheep are giving birth, the harvest is admirable, the cows are calving, the people are honest. It's just that cursed watermill!'

-'Come what may,' said a certain Raško Ćebo, the throatiest man in all Zarožje, 'let's get guns and spend the night...'

-'Hey... It's... Well, you know... Uh huh...,' murmured almost all the others out loud.

Then they got goose-bumps.[13] Those who were lying on their sides turned onto their stomachs, and those on their stomachs onto their sides.

Everyone thought a bit.

-'I maintain, brothers,' said *Kmet* Purko and scribbled furiously with the stick, 'that we look once more. That we find a miller as best we can...'

-'Hah!' jumped in Old Man Mirko. 'What kind of miller, God be with you? No one will do it for fear of his life!'

---

[13] The Serbian expression is "ants crawled over them".

-'Well, I don't know,' said Ćebo. 'It seems to me that we could spend the night ourselves...'

-'Well, I wouldn't spend the night,' interrupted a certain Vidoje Đilas, 'even if I had to grind wheat by pounding it in a post.'[14]

-'That's right, sonny, nor I,' agreed Old Man Mirko, 'not even if I had to pop popcorn and eat it instead of bread.'

-'Well, let's call the priest,' said a certain Srdan. 'Let him say a prayer...'

-'He's prayed, Srdan, and prayed,' answered Purko and kicked his legs, 'and it's never been of any use.'

-'I maintain, people,' said Old Man Mirko, 'that we build ourselves a different watermill. Thank God there are lots of streams; we have locations.'

-'And what will we do with this one?' asked Đilas.

-'Toss a torch in it,' said Old Man Mirko.

-'Admittedly it's better than having the whole world fall apart,' added Purko.

-'A sermon from the *Kmet*,' smirked Ćebo.

-'Don't start,' snapped Old Man Mirko, standing up.

-'Move aside,[15] Mirko, by God!' said Srdan. 'Whoever sows salt, grasshoppers pop up.'[16]

-'And did you stretch out a board, Srdan, huh?' smirked Ćebo.

-'Leave it alone, people!' shouted Purko, because he could see

---

[14] This refers to the ancient pre-milling practice of grinding wheat by pounding it in a tree stump.

[15] The expression "move aside" is spoken to someone who has said something distasteful, that brings bad luck, and who needs to take back his words.

[16] A proverb meaning that one reaps a bad reward for sowing bad deeds.

there would be havoc.

-'Even if you did stretch out a board,' said Old Man Mirko, 'at least you didn't dive into kids' wool like Đilas.'

-'Even if I did dive,' Đilas answered pointedly, 'at least I didn't shove walnuts into the loft with a pitchfork like you, Old Man.'

-'Don't bark!' Old Man Mirko lost his temper.

Everyone jumped to their feet.

The *Kmet* tried to calm them:

-'Quit it, folks! Let's speak like civilized people!'

Alas! Word by word they lashed out at one another, until a smack hit Ćebo on the back of the neck. Đilas had slapped him.

In a moment there was complete chaos. Everyone grabbed whatever was at hand, and struck… struck! All that could be heard was: 'No Ćebo… Stop, Old Man… Hold on, Srdan… Don't give in, *Kmet*!'

So they fought to their heart's content, then separated each to his own way, some bareheaded, some leaning on a shoulder, some feeling their ribs.

The *Kmet* entered into the house to wash, because his face was completely scratched.

And thus concluded that Zarožje gathering.

* * *

Early on St. Peter's Day[17] before sunrise, Strahinja sat near

---

[17] 12 July.

Zmajevac, the coldest spring in all Ovčina, which was right next to the village road below Živan's house. He sat there to rest a little and to light one up, and then to head onwards. He was ready to travel somewhere. On his belt were two pistols and a large knife. He had set his bag and sheep-skin vest beside him on the ground.

No sooner had he lit the pipe than Radojka appeared from above with jugs. She had gone to fetch water. When she saw Strahinja she jumped and turned around, frightened.

-'Hey, it's you, Radojka!' said Strahinja, then stood up and tossed his vest and bag across his shoulders.

-'And where are you off to so early?' asked Radojka, slowly and dejectedly.

-'Well, even I myself don't know,' answered Strahinja, shrugging his shoulders.

-'Are you still alive after the other day?'

-'Barely... and you?' asked Strahinja rather apprehensively.

-'Don't ask!' said Radojka and began to cry.

-'I already know... that horrid man,' said Strahinja, and waved his hand.

-'I don't have a life anymore,' Radojka continued through tears.

-'Neither do I,' added Strahinja. 'I'm going into the wide world, so whatever God grants...'

-'Where are you going, *bolan*?'[18] Radojka asked and looked at him.

---

[18] *Bolan*, a relatively untranslatable word typically used to address a male who is close, either in terms of family, friendship, or partnership. Today, it remains in widespread use in Bosnia and Herzegovina. The closest English equivalent may be the Australian use of the word "mate".

-'Anywhere… I'm going down to the Sava River Valley…'

-'Well good for you! And what will I do, poor me?'

-'Do what you know; endure! Certainly even that evil will finally come to an end.'

-'If at least you were here… If nothing else it would be easier for me if I could only see you every now and then…'

-'Oh Radojka, I love you as I love my own eyes. But what can I do? That horrid man won't let us get married. Old Man Sredoje told me everything. It's not even any use for me to mention it. I've thought twice about it. There's no other way, Radojka! I must leave here… At least until you get married… And after that, what happens, happens.'

-'But *bolan*, do you truly want to leave?'

-'By God, Radojka, truly.'

-'And your house?'

-'I've boarded up the house. It's better that it be overgrown with nettle and elderberry, if I can't be happy in it!' said Strahinja distantly.

-'I'm so wretched!' said Radojka, then, after waiting a bit, added: 'If you've decided to go, *bolan*, then don't go far! Here…you can even stay in Zarožje. You have your acquaintances there; you even have relatives, thank God. It seems to me Aunt Mirjana is your great aunt on your mother's side; she's from there.'

-'That's all so, Radojka, but I really can't… I want to go a bit further!'

Finally, Radojka began to beg him not to leave, or at least not to go far. But it was all in vain. Once Strahinja had made up his mind, there was nothing you could do to change it.

She began to cry as never before; she poured out her heart to Strahinja about Živan; she said that perhaps she would never marry if she wasn't destined to follow him; she bade farewell to him, hurried to fetch the water, then headed uphill towards home, crying…

Strahinja sighed, relit his pipe, exhaled two or three thick puffs of smoke, then hit the road heading downhill; he frequently glanced back at Radojka until she disappeared out of sight up into the orchard.

The further Strahinja moved away, the more difficult it was for him. Occasionally, something in his throat squeezed him so much that it seemed it would suffocate him. He felt how his eyes were full of tears, which rather angered him, so he furrowed his brow. He finished his pipe quicker than usual, then impulsively reached for his belt, pulled out tobacco, and quickly filled another…

When he reached the top of Desolate Hill he stood a bit and looked over at Ovčina. Živan's house could be seen, along with the fence around the house, the grove, and the meadow up above. It seemed to him that a child came from the house… but it was none other than Radojka. It seemed to him he could see she was still crying… Then he looked further down. The grove could be seen where Radojka frequently drove the sheep to graze, and where they had met and spoken sweetly. A bit further up the hill his house could be seen; from here it looked like a good-sized mushroom, no larger. There were some fields around, some vegetables, small pastures. All well-tended.

Strahinja had been an orphan since childhood, without a mother and father. He did have, however, some distant relatives both in Ovčina and Zarožje, but no one wanted to take him in or care for him. Only Aunt Mirjana sometimes asked about him and once gave him woolen socks… So ever since he was small, Strahinja began to roam around other people's houses. He served in Ovčina with the better landlords until he grew a bit and waxed stronger. Afterwards, he went to learn the builder's trade. He got along well with the Osat[19] builders and went with them even as far down as the Posavina[20] and built homes, outbuildings, and other structures for the wealthy Posavina dwellers. When he had thus saved a bit of money, he returned to Ovčina to the small inheritance that remained behind from his father. He tore down the old wooden cottage and built that small house all by himself. And there he lived as an industrious, humble and impecunious man…

Now it would all be completely abandoned. The village livestock would come and tear up the small field and trample the modest vegetables. The small cottage would be overgrown by weeds, and moss would envelope the white wood shingle.

Strahinja sighed; again something squeezed him sharply in his throat; again he drew in two or three puffs of thick smoke, then hurried downwards towards the area of Zarožje. He crossed over Desolate Hill. Before him appeared the deep Zarožje glens, the frequent brush and rocks, the rare fields and the even rarer houses.

---

[19] Osat, an area in the middle Drina River valley known for its builders who worked throughout Serbia, Croatia, and Bosnia during the 18th century.
[20] The Sava River valley.

The path led right through the middle of Zarožje, by the *Kmet*'s gate. Strahinja suddenly thought that it would be good to drop in for a bit on Purko and some other friends and bid them farewell. Who knew when they would see each other again? Those people had taken good care of him ever since he had returned from the building trade. Truth be told, everyone in Ovčina and the nearby villages loved Strahinja, except Živan... although a few people disapproved of him smoking tobacco while still a lad.

Back then, smoking was very rare there; you could see someone here and there with a pipe between the teeth, but only among the older people; and among the young men – never.

Strahinja looked back once more. Nothing more could be seen of Ovčina.

* * *

Around the mid-morning meal, Old Man Mirko, Ćebo, Srdan, Đilas, and other selectmen from the village appeared under the walnut tree in front of Purko's house. Some sat on the grass, while others stood. They spoke little and looked often at each other out of the corners of their eyes. It was as though they were ashamed that their previous meeting on St. John's Day had ended as it did. Even *Kmet* Purko seemed cautious. Since the people had arrived he still hadn't left the house. When, speak of the devil, out he came – carrying an earthen jug full of rakija.

-'Well, how have you been, good fellow?' asked Old Man Mirko.

-'Well… you know… the children…' *Kmet* Purko began to mutter, like a man trying to cover up something, then offered the jug to Mirko: 'Make a toast, by God.'

-'Brothers, may we have a prosperous day, prosperous work, and if God grants, may we see each other again healthy and flourishing!' Old Man Mirko said and raised the jug.

Purko, nonetheless, inquired after the health of Ćebo, Srdan, Đilas, and the others.

All acted as though they had neither eaten an onion nor smelled an onion.[21] 'Here, Ćebo,' said Old Man Mirko, offering him the jug. Ćebo offered two or three words as a toast, took a good draught, then handed it to Srdan, Srdan to Đilas, then to the man next to him, and so the jug went from hand to hand. When all had taken a turn and when the last one lowered the empty jug to the ground, *Kmet* Purko began:

-'Well, people, we've met often. Thank God, we've also quarreled often…'

-'And fought, by God,' Đilas added slowly.

-'But we've never parted in such discord,' continued Purko, acting as though he hadn't heard Đilas, 'as we did back on St. John's Day.'

-'By God, *Kmet*, forget it!' retorted Old Man Mirko. 'What happened, happened. Why did you bring it up?'

-'Well, that's what I say, it's just…' began the *Kmet*.

-'Ignore it!' agreed Đilas. 'Living people quarrel every now and

---

[21] An expression that means 'as though nothing had happened.'

then… they even fight… wonder of wonders! They're human!'

-'Yes, yes! That's right! Forget it *Kmet*, move on!' most of them shouted together.

The *Kmet* fell silent for a bit, than began:

-'What do you say, people? Shall we find a miller, or build a different watermill?'

-'Oh, that cursed watermill again?' grumbled someone.

-'Let's build a different one,' said Old Man Mirko.

-'Nah, let's find a miller!' said Srdan.

-'Let's mind it ourselves!' shouted Ćebo.

-'Nope! Let's tear this one down!' shouted Đilas.

-'No, we won't!' shouted some.

-'Let's!' yelled others.

-'Slow down, people, folks, brothers!' the *Kmet* tried to calm them.

-What do you mean "slow"?' squealed Old Man Mirko, turning completely red. 'Toss a torch into this one! Build another!'

-'Build it yourself!' snapped some. 'Really, a torch?'

-'Old Man Mirko is right!' yelled others.

-'Hey, people, brothers!' the *Kmet* tried to pacify them.

An absolute tumult arose. It couldn't be known who said what. The *Kmet* waved his arms, ran from one to the other calming them…

Then a man appeared on the road above. His bag was over his shoulder and he hurried downhill.

-'Who could that be?' wondered the *Kmet*.

Everyone wondered and looked upward.

-'It seems to me it's Strahinja,' said Ćebo.

-'Which Strahinja?' asked Old Man Mirko.

-'Why ours, from Ovčina!' exclaimed Ćebo.

-'By God, it is!' added Đilas.

-'What's he want in Zarožje?' asked someone.

-'Well, thank God he has someone to come to,' said the *Kmet*.

Then Strahinja arrived down at Purko's gate.

-'Strahinja, brother!' the *Kmet* summoned him. 'If God so grants, stop by here a little.

-'Stop by a little, Strahinja, stop by!' hollered Ćebo.

-'Come on, come on, brother!' agreed the others.

-'Rest a little,' added the *Kmet*.

Strahinja entered the gate and greeted them:

-'May God be with you!'[22]

-'Hey Strahinja, drink a little!' said Srdan, and handed him the jug. 'You must be tired.'

-'Well, I guess I am,' answered Strahinja, and took the jug and sat down among them.

-'Where did you come from?' inquired the *Kmet*.

-'From home,' said Strahinja tipping the jug. Then he quickly stopped, smiled a bit, and asked: 'Is this what you offer a traveler?'

-'It isn't empty, is it?' asked Ćebo.

-'By God it is,' said the *Kmet*, taking the jug and shaking it; then he quickly ran into the house.

-'Do you plan to go far?' asked Old Man Mirko.

---

[22] '*Pomozi Bog*,' a standard Serbian greeting.

-'Far away, by God,' answered Strahinja seriously.

-'Oh? And how far?'

-'Maybe even all the way to Posavina.'

-'To Posavina…' nearly everyone exclaimed in astonishment.

-'And why on earth?' asked the *Kmet*, who just at that moment brought rakija in the jug.

-'I must, Purko,' Strahinja said and sighed.

Everyone looked at him a bit incredulously.

Strahinja took a drink, pulled a pipe from his belt and lit it, then asked:

-'It seems to me that you are deliberating about something here.'

-'Oh, we are agonizing,' said Đilas.

-'Oh? And why?' asked Strahinja, expelling a puff of smoke.

-'We are without a miller,' replied Purko. 'You can't find a single one.'

-'No one dares, brother, no one dares.' Ćebo jumped in.

-'Something strange is strangling people,' continued Purko. 'Not a single miller can endure. At dusk, he is hale and whole, and when it dawns, he is dead.'

-'Well, they're also talking about it over in Ovčina,' said Strahinja, and began to brood over something.

-'The village is large,' responded Srdan, 'and there's only one watermill.'

-'And there's an abomination in it,' added Old Man Mirko.

-'But we lack the skill, by God' said the *Kmet*, 'to build another.'

-'And you can't find a brave man…,' said Ćebo.

-'You know what, people?' said Strahinja boldly.

-'What? What? What?' almost everyone shouted, curiously.

-'If you'd like, I will be your miller.'

-'You? God be with you! Move aside!' Many cried out in disbelief.

-'Yes. I… at least for one night,' answered Strahinja forcefully.

-'Stop it, brother,' Purko said to him. 'Don't joke.'

-'But you're going to Posavina,' said Old Man Mirko.

-I'm not… I changed my mind!' Strahinja answered and expelled two puffs of smoke, one after the other. 'I would be very pleased to look after your watermill, even if for only one night.'

-'Oh, Strahinja,' Purko answered again. 'We know you, we love you… so we aren't pleased…'

But Strahinja became stubborn and wouldn't relent in the least!

When the *Zarožani* saw that they couldn't change his mind, they acquiesced… Let him, if he really wanted to so badly. He told them only that they should prepare lots of wheat so that the watermill could grind all night, and not to worry about him.

The *Zarožani* parted, shaking their heads skeptically and shrugging their shoulders.

Strahinja remained at Purko's. Purko kept him for lunch and to be his guest until dark, even though it was a holiday, St. Peter's Day. In the evening he would take him to the watermill…

* * *

The vale where the Zarožje watermill lies is truly horrifying. To the one side is a thick forest, and by day it is dark within, not to mention by night. To the other side are barren rocks and stones. The stream twists down under the side where the forest lies; here and there it murmurs across wide flat rocks into whirlpools; here and there its winds between boulders as large as a haystack. The watermill is right underneath one such boulder, stuck to it like a swallow's nest.

It had long since fallen dark. Pitch-black -- as thick as dough. The silent time. Now and then down below the watermill at the ford, the water burbled sharply. Nothing could be heard anywhere. Except here and there a Nightjar sang[23] near the stream, or an owl screeched in the forest, or from the village above some dog could be heard barking two or three times and then falling silent.

Strahinja stoked the fire in the watermill. He poured a bag of wheat into the hopper; two others stood ready. He went out once more and checked whether all was well with the catch tub, adjusted the top stone to grind fine, and pushed the flour into the bin.

Then he dragged in some sort of a large log, long as a man is tall. He placed it next to the fire and shoved a small stump underneath one end, then covered and arranged it as though someone were lying there.

When he had arranged everything, he slowly climbed up to the loft, which was comprised of several boards right above the door. He pulled out both pistols, into each of which he loaded a piece of steel and one *marjaš*,[24] cocked them and placed them in front of him, then

---

[23] A crepuscular and nocturnal bird (*caprimulgus europaeus*).
[24] A Turkish coin worth about 2 groš (Austrian Groschen).

stretched out on his stomach in the loft and waited for what would happen…

Then fell the deaf period. Neither a Nightjar nor an owl could be heard any more. Only the grain shoe clacking, the water murmuring in a spray[25] under the watermill, and… nothing else.

Until at once a tall man with a face as red as blood entered the watermill; he entered silently… it could be said that the door didn't even open. He had tossed across his shoulders a linen shroud that dropped down his back all the way to his heels.[26] He slowly approached the bin, shoved his hand in and took a little flour, examined it in his palm, then tossed it back into the bin.

Strahinja slowly took both pistols and made ready; he had completely stopped breathing to conceal himself.

The man sat down next to the fire. He sat for a bit, and all the while watched the log from the corner of his eye, then arose easily, approached the log, and at once began to choke it. But he quickly jumped back and stopped; surprised it could be said. He stood like that, just stood, then bellowed so that the entire watermill reverberated:

-'Oh, Sava Savanović! For 90 years you've been a vampire, and you've never gone without supper as you have this evening!'

---

[25] This refers to *"omaja"*, the jet of water that emerges from under the waterwheel. Folk tradition imbues this water with mystical properties. The water is collected the evening before St. George's Day (Đurđevdan, 6 May) and placed in jugs and bottles together with sprigs of dogwood, pussy willow, cherry plum, and blossoms. The next morning it is sprinkled on the members of the household to ensure health and prosperity in the upcoming year.

[26] In South Slav folklore, a vampire's power resides in its burial shroud, which it typically wears draped around its neck and shoulders. If the vampire loses this shroud, then it loses any special powers.

As soon as he said this, Strahinja aimed both pistols and Bang! Bang! Something cried out and groaned a little. The smoke cleared. There was nothing anywhere.

Strahinja slowly climbed down from above, stirred the fire and looked at the door; it was wide open. He took a torch in one hand and a knife in the other, then went outside; he looked everywhere around the watermill – there was nothing anywhere! He returned inside again, closed the door most of the way, poured flour from the bin into a sack, and poured another one into the hopper. He loaded the pistols and lit a pipe – he wanted to wait until the sun rose. Even though he was courageous, he was still rather frightened.

Then the cock crowed in the village. Strahinja felt very relieved. All was well; there was now nothing to fear.

* * *

And so Strahinja greeted the dawn, hale and whole.

He was just getting ready to leave the watermill and head up to the village, when the *Zarožani* appeared -- the same ones who had been at the meeting, and the *Kmet* with them.

For as long as they could remember, they had probably never been so startled as when they found Strahinja alive.

-'Oh, by God, are you really alive?' they all shouted aloud in wonderment.

-'I'm alive, yeah,' Strahinja answered somewhat carelessly.

-'Well what happened brother? Tell us, tell us!' Everyone flocked around, suffocating from curiosity to hear the miracle of how he had remained alive.

Just when Strahinja had begun to tell them everything as it had occurred, the entire village headed down from above, even some old women and wives. They all grouped around him, filling the watermill and standing in front of the door.

As he told them what happened, they were astonished and shook their heads, crying:

-'Oh, brother, by God!'

-'How strange, people!'

-'Oh, God be with us!'

But when he told them what the vampire had shouted, everyone began to ponder. They kept silent for a long time. No one there was capable of saying anything clever.

-'By God, that's right!' Old Man Mirko began. 'Ever since I remember, we haven't been able to keep a single miller, and also lots of people have died in the village.'

-'Well, does anyone know any Sava Savanović?' asked Purko.

-'Nope... no one knows!' shouted almost all the people.

The *Zarožani* pondered again.

An old woman pushed her way in, grey as a sheep, and squawked in a grandmotherly fashion:

-'Children, do you know who will know this the best?'

-'Who, who, who?' cried many of them, curiously.

-'No one other than Grandma Mirjana.'[27]

---

[27] In Zarožje, oral tradition holds that Mirjana lived to be 110 or 120 years old.

-'Which Mirjana?' asked Purko.

-'Why the one from Ovčina,' said the old woman and turned towards Strahinja. 'She's one of your relatives, sonny.'

-'She is,' replied Strahinja carelessly, and added: 'perhaps she will know best…'

-'I hadn't even learned to walk,' continued the old woman, 'when Mirjana got married in Ovčina. If she doesn't know, no one knows.'

-'Well let's call Mirjana,' said Purko. 'Someone should go to Ovčina right now.'

-'But she's gone blind,' said Strahinja.

-'And she's gone deaf,' added Ćebo.

-'And she's lame,' said Old Man Mirko.

-'Well then, let's go to her,' said the *Kmet*.

-'Let's go, let's go to Mirjana!' many shouted.

-'We'll be in Ovčina by lunchtime,' shouted Ćebo and Srdan.

-'We can return by dark,' added Đilas.

-'And I say we go tomorrow,' said Old Man Mirko.

-'Nope… Better today… Now… Right away!' A tumult arose.

-'Stop, people!' shouted the *Kmet*. 'And I say today is better! Now let's go up to my house and have a drink… and this man is tired (here the *Kmet* gestured towards Strahinja). And we could use it…'

And so, all the more select *Zarožani* headed up to the village to the *Kmet*'s house. The rest of the people went each their own way, amazed at Strahinja's bravery.

The *Kmet* and Strahinja lagged behind a bit and continued the conversation.

-'By your faith, Strahinja, tell me truly what I am about to ask you.'

-'Of course, Purko, I will, but only if it's something I can tell.'

-'Tell me straight, what has driven you away from home? We are, thank God, good friends and acquaintances from way back. I love you like a son... We all love you here in the village... I would really like it if you told me if misfortune has found you.'

Strahinja fell silent for a bit, then said:

-'Alright, Purko, I can tell you: but it will be difficult for you to help me... I'll tell you so that it is a bit easier on me. You probably know about our *Kmet*.'

-'Živan Dušman? Well do I know him. We are *Kum*[28] to each other in some manner... Last year you made him *Kmet* there.'

-'And do you know his Radojka?'

-'I do. An honest girl... only her father is a bit of a blackguard.'

-'You see, Purko,' continued Strahinja, looking ahead, 'I long ago became fond of that girl.'

-'I heard about that... it's already being talked about here ... So Živan is fighting, won't give in?'

-'He won't... just before St. John's Day[29] I asked Old Man Sredoje to go to Živan and to raise it.'

-'So what happened, good fellow?'

-'Nothing! Živan became furious, and as he's already horrid, he

---

[28] A *Kum* denotes a special traditional relationship usually connected to vital rituals, such as birth, baptism, and marriage. Thus a *Kum* could be a godfather, a best man, or a baptismal *Kum*, among others. Glišić does not specify the context, although later in the story it becomes clear that Purko is godfather to Radojka.
[29] July 7th.

almost got in a fight with Sredoje.'

-'Just look at that piece of bad luck! Just wait until I go there – I'll cut him into pieces and shake him by the ears!' said Purko, almost bitterly. 'And you?'

-'When Sredoje told me, something darkened before my eyes. The entire night I couldn't shut my eyes. I struggled with myself about everything. Finally I decided to go into the wide world...'

-'Oh Strahinja, you are crazy! What kind of wide world? It's a wonder, by God, that he doesn't give her to you! There are, thank God, also some good girls here among us...'

-'No, Purko,' replied Strahinja distantly. 'Since St. John's Day I've grown to hate that village, and the people, and my house, and everything... I really don't feel like living anymore.'

Purko realized that Strahinja had left Ovčina because of his deep despair; that he had intentionally demanded to mind the Zarožje watermill in order to die there, and that he would truly go off into the world, and perhaps meet his ruin somewhere... He began to admonish and dissuade him.

He barely convinced him to stay for at a few days with him in Zarožje until they found Sava Savanović; and afterwards to see if he could somehow help him obtain approval to wed Radojka, if she was that dear to him, even if they had to abduct her from Živan.

And while they were talking, they arrived up in front of the house.

All the select *Zarožani* who had come up from the watermill were already there. Purko immediately brought out rakija, and all took turns with a drink or two. Then they agreed that Purko, Old Man Mirko, and Raško Ćebo go to Ovčina and ask Grandma Mirjana if she knew whether there had ever been a Sava Savanović in Zarožje.

* * *

Noon had already long passed. In front of the Mirjanić house in Ovčina an old, ancient grandmother sat in the shade on a small throw rug. Her chin and knees had already met up and she looked like a specter. Her third set of teeth had long ago appeared.[30]

That was Grandma Mirjana. In the village some called her 'Grandma Mirjana,' and some 'Aunt Mirjana.' Because of her the house was called the house of *Mirjanića*, and all in the household *Mirjanići*.[31]

And so, the old woman sat in the shade on some throw rug; it was a holiday and they had carried her outside in front of the house for a bit. On working days the old woman normally didn't move from the hearth.

Children were working around the house.

Then the *Zarožani* opened the gate and entered.

While still at the gate, *Kmet* Purko shouted:

-'Householder! Is there anyone home?'

-'There is, there is,' answered Srećko the elder of the house, the great-grandson of Mirjana, and he ran from the house.

---

[30] She had lost all her teeth.

[31] It was common practice among the South Slavs to give a nickname to a household, and then use it instead of the family name for all the members of that household.

-'Can you receive guests, Srećko?' asked Old Man Mirko.

-'Good ones? At any hour!' answered Srećko coming out to greet them.

Here they greeted each other well, as civilized people and friends.

Srećko asked them what pleasantness brought them to him in Ovčina. The *Zarožani* related to him everything that had happened there the previous evening and for what reason they came. Srećko laughed and told them:

-'Here's Grandma Mirjana. You ask her.'

-'Go on Purko, you start,' said Old Man Mirko.

-'No way, Mirko,' retorted Purko, 'you do it.'

-'Well alright then, I will, if there's no-one else,' said Old Man Mirko, and all drew nearer before the old lady.

Mirko coughed, then shouted:

-'Mirjana.'

The old woman was silent.

-'She doesn't hear,' said Srećko, and laughed. 'Shout better, Old Man Mirko.'

-'I can't do any better,' answered Old Man Mirko. 'You do it, Purko!'

-'Oooh, Mirjana!!' shouted Purko at the top of his lungs.

The old woman didn't budge.

-'Louder, louder, Purko,' said Srećko.

-'Even I can't do any better,' answered Purko. 'Ćebo, you holler! You're the throatiest man in Zarožje, thank God!

-'Mirjana!' shouted Ćebo as loud as he could; even the dogs were startled, and they barked from somewhere behind the house.

-'Yes, sonny,' responded grandma Mirjana slowly, raising her head a little.

-'Do you know of a Sava Savanović?,' shouted Ćebo again.

-'What did you say, sonny?' asked the old woman slowly.

-'Do you know a Sava Savanović?' Ćebo yelled.

-'Where are you from, children?' asked the old woman.

-'From Zarožje,' yelled Ćebo.

-'Huh?' said the old woman, not hearing well.

-'Boy, is she ever deaf!' said Ćebo to the company, then cleared his throat and opened his mouth as wide as he could: 'From Zarožje!' The dogs again barked and howled behind the house.

-'Go on, go on,' said the old woman slowly, as though she was thinking a little about what they had asked her, and answered: 'and who is that, sonny?'

-'Sava Savanović!' thundered Ćebo and turned completely red from the intense exertion.

-'I know, children,' answered the old woman. 'I barely remember him. He was an evil man.'

-'And where is he buried?' bellowed Ćebo again.

-'In Crooked Ravine, beneath a spreading elm…' said the old woman, and again lowered her head.

The *Zarožani* pondered mightily.

In Zarožje there are, thank God, lots of ravines, both straight and crooked, and lots of spreading elms; but no one could remember exactly where that particular Crooked Ravine and spreading elm were. Even if they finally found the ravine, what about the elm? Perhaps its roots weren't even there... It had been so long since it was last whole that it was no joke.

They continued to ask grandma Mirjana whether she could say approximately where it was. Alas. The old woman couldn't hear anything. Ćebo had gone hoarse, and none of the others could shout like him. Not even Srećko was able to tell them anything. He didn't recall that Grandma Mirjana had ever said anything about it.

When they could no longer learn anything more from the old woman, they arose and left.

As they were leaving at the gate, *Kmet* Purko said:

-'There's no use, people, we'll just have to find that ravine, right?'

-'Yup, exactly,' said Old Man Mirko.

-'And settle down for once!' added Ćebo hoarsely.

-'So where will we find a black horse -- an ungelded horse -- and holy water?' asked Mirko.

-'By God, that's right,' said Purko. 'We'll need that.'

-'I have holy water,' said Ćebo, 'but a black horse?'

-'I have a small black horse,' said Old Man Mirko, 'but he's a gelding. And your blackie, Purko, don't you have one?'

-'Mine is also gelded,' said Purko. 'It seems to me that no one in Zarožje has a stallion.'

'As long as we're in Ovčina, let's ask,' said Old Man Mirko.

'You speak truly, by God,' agreed Purko. 'My *Kum*, Živan, has one. We could stop by along the way to ask... He'll probably give it to me. You go home and call the people together so we can agree what to do.'

Purko said this, then turned and headed on some path towards Živan's house. Old Man Mirko and Ćebo went back to Zarožje...

* * *

Živan had just risen, because the chill had dissipated, the sun had begun to warm up, and the heat had awakened him; when Purko appeared.

-'May God be with you,' called Purko still from a distance. 'Are you resting?'

-'That's right, yeah,' answered Živan yawning and groggy. 'I laid down a little, then this devilish heat... Aah! What are you doing here, *Kum*?'

-'I came down from the village,' answered Purko and sat down. 'I went with some people to *Mirjanića* on some business.'

-'I know, to ask Grandma Mirjana...' said Živan, then laughed and yawned.

Purko looked at him somewhat astonished, then smiled and said:

-'When did you find out?'

-'I'm not *Kmet* for nothing, thank God.'

-'You have, it seems to me, a black stallion?' asked Purko, not wanting to prolong the conversation.

-'I do. And what do you want with it?'

-'Well, we need it... you know...'

-'You *Zarožani* are really crazy,' said Živan, then laughed again.

'You're seeking a vampire! And who was it that spent the night in the watermill?'

-'Well, Strahinja,' said Purko, and to move the conversation along, he asked: 'By God, *Kum*, why did you drive off that fellow?'

-'Who, *Kum*?'

-'Why Strahinja!'

-'Well, no one chased him away,' answered Živan and yawned once more.

-'Well, you drove him off!'

-'Well!' said Živan and came closer a bit. 'And so what?'

-'Why don't you give the lad the girl?'

-'Really, to him?' shouted Živan and jumped up. 'To that trash, who's been stuffing tobacco into a pipe since he fell out of diapers? Now *Kum*, you've lost your mind!'

-'*Kum*!' shouted Purko and jumped to his feet. 'Come to your senses, I'm a *Kmet*!'

-'And I'm a *Kmet*!' Živan huffed at him. 'If that's why you came to me, then go freely! There's the gate!'

-'Don't be like that *Kum*, don't,' Purko began more mildly. 'That lad isn't to be taken lightly. When children love each other and are fond of each other, then let them... they should get married.'

-'Did you hear me, *Kum*?' said Živan and stood directly in Purko's face. 'I won't give her to him, even if she braids grey hair!'[32]

-'*Kum*, don't condemn me!' said Purko. He fell silent for a bit, then asked: 'And you really won't give her?'

---

[32] Becomes old and grey.

-'Don't ever mention it to me again!' said Živan distantly. 'Unless you want us to quarrel.'

-'As you wish,' said Purko and shrugged his shoulders. 'Just so you don't have regrets. It's always better to do something by grace than by force.'

-'Child!' shouted Živan, not listening to what Purko said.

-'I'm listening, sir,' answered some small boy from the house.

-'Go with the *Kum* down to the pasture. Catch the black stallion, give it to him and let him take it.'

The little boy ran from the house, then went ahead to the pasture.

-Hey, I'm going too, *Kum*,' said Purko. 'I need to hurry home so that the people don't wait for me.'

-'Take care of my horse, *Kum*!' bade Živan, and headed inside the house. 'I wouldn't give it to anyone else for my head.'

-'Many thanks, *Kum*! May you have health! Remember what I told you,' said Purko and headed downward after the small boy.

Živan simply turned around, stared at him and mumbled something…

Purko took Živan's black horse and headed slowly towards Zarožje.

* * *

At dawn the next day almost all the *Zarožani* gathered under the walnut tree in front of Purko's house. Everything was ready that they had agreed on the previous evening. Old Man Mirko had gone to the priest and asked him to set forth with them; it would be useful for him to say a prayer. Purko brought Živan's black horse without marks, still ungelded. Đilas had cut a stake of black hawthorn[33] and sharpened it so that it couldn't be better. Ćebo brought a small flask with holy water. Some brought picks and mattocks.

When the sun had already bounced off the spear,[34] all the people set out to find Crooked Ravine and the spreading elm. They entered one ravine that was, truth be told, rather crooked, but there was no elm, and it wasn't known that there could ever have been any kind of tree there. That wasn't it!

They went to another. In it were elms, scattered and spreading; but again the ravine wasn't crooked; rather it ran straight, as though cut precisely with a thread. That wasn't it either!

They went to a third ravine. Here again were many spreading trees, but not a single one was an elm; rather beeches or other types of trees. The ravine was as crooked as crooked could be, but what was the use when there wasn't an elm? That wasn't it either!

They entered a fourth ravine. It was crooked and entirely full of spreading elms, but small ones; the thickest was barely 20 years old, much less 90. That wasn't it either!

The *Zarožani* had already begun to lose all hope; they couldn't find it – all their troubles were in vain. Let's go see one more ravine. Truly, it was far away, but since they had already set off – well, why

[33] According to South Slav folklore and beliefs, a vampire must be killed with a hawthorn stake. The symbolism was enriched by the belief that Christ's crown of thorns was made from hawthorn branches. Hawthorn trees also emit trimethylene, which attracts butterflies.
[34] The sundial had crossed the halfway mark, i.e., noon had passed.

not?

They climbed over a cliff, then descended into some wide, enormous ravine. It seemed to them to be quite crooked. Just when they entered into it they came upon an elm – fat, gigantic; you could say it was 100 years old. There were almost no other trees, just here and there a bush or a thorn plant. But there were several thick stumps, some of them burned out, some already rotten – it was almost all deadwood.

The *Zarožani* wandered around the ravine, and wandered; here there was also nothing. They had already begun to halt from exhaustion – they were falling off their feet.

-'Stop, people,' shouted Purko, 'let's rest our souls a bit. This is killing us!'

-'You're right, brothers, we're really dying,' said Old Man Mirko, 'and in vain.'

-'Well, brothers, did you hear Grandma Mirjana well?' asked the *Kmet*, doubtfully. 'Didn't she say precisely "in Crooked Ravine under the spreading elm"?'

-'We heard, brother, just as you did; exactly that!' Ćebo and Old Man Mirko responded together.

-'Well, you can't find it, there's no use,' said the *Kmet* completely in despair. 'Whoa, calm down, he's breaking loose!' He then promptly shouted at the black horse, which had started neighing and begun to dig with his hoof.

The horse stopped a bit, then dug again, first with one hoof, then with the other; he sniffed the earth and whinnied. Purko pulled him by the bridle and tried to soothe him, but he wouldn't settle down!

-'Well, what's the matter with him now?' shouted the *Kmet*, already irate, and began to beat the horse spuriously with a stick.

The horse settled down a bit, then again began to dig, snort, and sniff.

-'Hey *Kmet*, look at that!' said Strahinja.

-'What?'

-'Well, it seems to me that there is something rotten, something wooden... there where the horse is digging!'

'There is, by God!' said the *Kmet* and went to take a closer look.

Everyone crowded around to see.

-'Somebody dig with a pick!' said Old Man Mirko.

One man approached, swung several times, and truly a stump of sorts appeared. The horse snorted more and more and dug with its hoof.

-'It's here! It's here!' everyone shouted, somewhat frightened.

-'Child, give me some of that deadwood!' said Old Man Mirko.

The man who had been digging with a pick took some of the rotten wood from the stump and handed it to the old man. The old man examined it and said:

-'It's elm, by God! Truly, I would swear on my life that it's the stump of that spreading elm.'

-'It could be,' said someone. 'Look at where the horse is digging with its hoof and snorting.'

-'And this is the ravine,' continued the old man, 'the oldest, it seems to me. Not one of the others is this deep and broad.'

-'Okay, people, let's dig here!' said the *Kmet.*

-'Let's dig!' they all cried.

Those with picks and mattocks gathered and began digging energetically. They unearthed an enormous stump at the spot and dug further. Already, the sun had begun to set and there was still nothing. They were all close to halting, but decided to dig a bit more, and if there was nothing, then they would go home. They hadn't swung the pick more than two or three times, when some sort of planks appeared. All gathered round to see. That's it! The deeper they went, the more the planks stood out. Finally it was identified as a grave. Slowly, they cleared the earth everywhere around the planks and prepared to lift the lid.

Ćebo brought the holy water. The priest put on the *epitrachelion*[35] and opened the prayer book. Đilas rolled up his sleeves, took the Hawthorn stake and readied himself.

-'Look well,' said Old Man Mirko, 'that you don't spatter any blood on us or on yourself. And you, Ćebo, pour the holy water immediately. Watch out that a male butterfly[36] doesn't fly out.'

The *Kmet* shouted at those who were digging:

-'Now grab a part of the lid and lift it slowly with the picks.'

They did so. And there was a sight to see! A man lay whole and

---

[35] The stole worn around the neck of an Eastern Orthodox priest while performing his duties.

[36] In South Slav folklore, the human soul emerges from the mouth of the deceased in the form of a butterfly. So too, vampires are thought to turn into butterflies, not bats. Butterflies are attracted to graves and decomposing bodies, due to the trimethylene emitted by decomposing corpses. Hawthorn trees also emit trimethylene, which causes butterflies to cluster on them.

unspoiled, as though they had lowered him in there yesterday. Except that he had one leg crossed over the other, and his arms stretched out at his sides, bloated as a wineskin, completely red it seemed, as though entirely from blood, one eye shut and the other open. On his fingers they recognized two gunshot wounds, but both were almost completely healed.

Đilas extended the stake and impaled the vampire in the middle of the chest.

-'Holy water, Ćebo!' shouted Purko.

In the rush Ćebo didn't pour it exactly in the mouth, but rather splashed it on his face. In that instant a wisp of some sort of fog escaped from the vampire's mouth, a true butterfly, and flew off somewhere.

-'Aaaa, the butterfly's getting away!' many people shouted.

-'What in God's name did you do, Ćebo?'

The priest read a prayer over the vampire, then they immediately buried him. On the grave they piled stones, logs, and all sorts of thorns -- mostly hawthorn.

The *Zarožani* only just returned to their homes by dusk, pleased that they had found the vampire Sava and stopped him in that manner. True, the butterfly[37] had gotten away from them, but they didn't care. It couldn't hurt grown people.

* * *

[37] The word *"leptirak"* is used, denoting a large male butterfly.

Such festivity, such merriment, had not taken place in Zarožje in a long time, as took place on that Friday, St. Paul's Day,[38] and the next day, Saturday, when the *Zarožani* returned from Crooked Ravine hungry and tired with their *Kmet* and priest.

The *Kmet* invited them all to his home for a drink. There they drank, ate, and sang. There they drank to the souls of all the millers who had, up until then, been found dead in the Zarožje watermill. There they drank to the health of the priest, the *Kmet*, Strahinja, and all of Zarožje. There they fired off guns with each toast.

Evening had long since passed, and it was now some hour of the night. The guests were celebrating in front of the house; moonlight bright as day, summer, the people were enjoying sitting. Some wished to go. Purko stopped them.

-'Sit down, people! Sit, Mirko, Ćebo! Have another one! Tomorrow is Sunday. There isn't any sort of work waiting for us. Come on, Father, make a toast!'

-'It's fine, it's fine, right,' stuttered the priest, then took a glass, stood up as though he wished to say something, then drank it and sat down.

The Zarožje priest wasn't particularly eloquent, and whenever he found himself at some sort of festivity with people, something seemed to take his tongue, and he was unable to say anything other than "It's fine, it's fine, right".'

-'You do it, Old Man Mirko,' said Purko. 'Stand in for our priest. Make a toast!'

---

[38] July 13th.

-'Here's to the health of our Strahinja!' began Old Man Mirko, taking a glass. 'First to his head – his wife...'

-'Uuhaa, Old Man Mirko! Don't be foolish! He still doesn't have a wife!' shouted everyone, laughing.

-'That's right, by God!' said Mirko. 'Look, I've muddled something. Well, he'll have one if he doesn't!' The old man spoke sincerely because he felt bad that he had muddled things.

-'Of course! That's right! He'll have one if he doesn't!' shouted nearly everybody.

-'I just wonder about that crazy Živan,' said Purko as an aside, 'Why doesn't he give him the girl?'

-'You mean that fella from Ovčina?' asked Old Man Mirko.

-'And he, of course... when they love and cherish each other,' continued Purko, 'Why don't they get hitched?'

-'Move aside, Purko!' said Strahinja, dismissing him with a wave of his hand.

-'What do you mean "move aside"?' continued Purko, coming further into the firelight. 'Here in Zarožje anyone would give you a girl, some a daughter, some a niece, isn't that right, brothers?'

-'It is, it is... Strahinja is a valiant lad... Strahinja is ours!' shouted almost everyone.

-'And that blackguard wouldn't even let it be mentioned! Why, out of deep despair the fellow has left his house and everything, and intends to go into the wide world.'

-'Well, are you crazy?' Ćebo jumped in, turning to Strahinja. 'If the girl wants only you, find some people and steal her away!'

40

-'Leave it alone, Ćebo,' Strahinja said to him. 'I don't want to…'

-'What don't you want to do?' Srdan jumped in. 'Here, we'll go with you!'

-'By God we will!' agreed Ćebo. 'Here, I'll be first. Does anyone else want to?'

-'I will!' shouted Đilas.

-'And I… and I!' shouted many of them, even Old Man Mirko.

-'Well, if you're going, Old Man Mirko, then I will too' said Purko.

-'Oh, people! Purko! Ćebo!' shouted Strahinja to calm them down. 'Stop and let's think this through some more! Let's see when…'

-'Right away! That's right! Immediately!' everyone shouted in the turmoil.

-'It's a sin…' Strahinja began to say.

-'There's nothing sinful here!' responded Ćebo, not letting him speak. 'Here's the priest, let's ask him!'

-'Father, is it a sin to kidnap a girl?' asked Purko.

-'It's fine, it's fine, right,' answered the priest, and his eyebrows appeared to flutter.

-'And when the lad is valiant, honest?' responded Old Man Mirko turning to the priest.

-'It's fine, it's fine, right!'

-'And when the girl cherishes him?' continued Purko.

-'It's fine, it's fine, right!' the priest answered, first one way, then another.

-'Well, if it's fine, then let's go, brothers!' shouted Ćebo. Come on, Strahinja!'

Strahinja pleaded to stop them somehow. He implored them to desist, to not agitate the people; he told them he would rather go away anywhere than to have blood spilled because of him. But it was all in vain. Who can dissuade *Zarožani* when they've made up their minds?

And so they chose: Ćebo, Srdan, Đilas, Old Man Mirko, *Kmet* Purko and another two or three short-tempered lads. They brought guns, just in case they came across trouble. Strahinja had nowhere to go, so he agreed to accompany them.

The *Kmet* turned to the guests who had remained:

-'You, brothers, sit here, eat and drink what God has given you.'

-'We will, we will Purko! Thank you!' they shouted.

-'When the first cocks crow,' Purko continued, 'by the Grace of God, we'll be here with the bride.

-'And so may it be! May God grant it!' answered the guests simultaneously.

-'And be ready, brothers; if it comes to trouble, you will aid us in our trouble! To your health, brothers!' finished Purko.

-'We will, brother! Don't gather worries! To your health!' all the guests shouted after him.

-'It's fine, it's fine, right' the priest's voice was heard among theirs.

And then the *Kmet* departed with the company.

* * *

They arrived quickly before Živan's gate in Ovčina. There they came to a halt to agree what they would do and how.

They immediately agreed. Strahinja and Ćebo jumped the woven wooden fence, slowly removed an enormous stone that had been propped against the gate, and opened it wide. Purko, Old Man Mirko and the others remained at the gate. Strahinja and Ćebo stole up to the outbuilding,[39] which was a good arm's throw from the house, and waited.

-'Do you know for certain that she's in the out-building?' asked Ćebo, whispering.

-'That's what she told me earlier,' answered Strahinja.

-'What about Živan and the other members of the household?'

-'They always sleep in the house.'

-'Then call her, quickly!' whispered Ćebo, and moved behind the outbuilding.

Strahinja slowly stole up to the very door of the outbuilding, concealed himself a bit behind an empty barrel that was there, and called quietly:

-'Radojka! Radojka!'

She didn't respond.

Strahinja listened. Nothing could be heard. He fell silent for a bit, then called again:

---

[39] The traditional Serbian farm had a dual purpose outbuilding (*vajat*). Its primary function was to store food and equipment. Its secondary function was to serve as sleeping quarters for newlyweds so that their conjugal activities would not disturb the other members of the typical four-generation household.

-'Radojka! Radojka!'

-'Who is it?' A sleepy female voice was heard from inside.

-'It is I... Strahinja! Come out for a bit!' Strahinja answered quickly and brought his ear to the door.

Inside, some rustling was heard, then a silent step, then the door opened slowly and Radojka emerged, completely dressed and with shoes on.

-'What are you doing here at this hour?' she asked Strahinja, whispering.

-'Well, I came!' Strahinja began, then added: 'Well look here! When did you find time to get dressed and put on your shoes?'

-'Don't ask, my Strahinja!' answered Radojka, quieter still. 'Poppa won't let me live! I entered into this deserted outbuilding. I fell on the bed dressed as you see me now and cried and cried... I thought I would cry my eyes out. Then slumber overcame me and I fell asleep. And then you called...'

-'So he's tormenting you just because of me?'

-'Truly, Strahinja, I wanted to jump in the water[40] or close my eyes, but where can I flee to? It can't be endured any longer.'

-'Well come on, Radojka, we came precisely...'

-'You're taking all day!' whispered Ćebo, who had stolen up on them.

-'Who is that?' asked Radojka, and drew back a little.

-'Don't be afraid!' Strahinja assured her. 'He's our acquaintance from Zarožje. Come on, Radojka!'

---

[40] To commit suicide by drowning.

-'But *bolan*, Strahinja, how can I...?' She began to act as though she would hesitate.

-'Easy! Come with us!' whispered Ćebo quickly. 'With people good and honest... Come on, come on! Quickly! Before they notice us...'

Radojka began to say something again, but Strahinja and Ćebo pressed her: 'Come on, come on!' and almost not knowing how, she emerged from the out-building and hurried off with them.

Of all the bad luck! In her hurry and distress Radojka bumped into the barrel, which rolled down the hill, thudding and hitting, here a tree and there a rock.

-'Alas, what did you do?' said Ćebo. 'You're waking the children! Run, Run!'

And all three fled as fast as they could towards the gate...

But God gives nothing for free. Živan flew out in front of the house and shouted:

-'Thieves! Bring the guns! Don't let them get away!'

Two others emerged from the house. A gun thundered.

The *Zarožani* began to run precipitously, simply to distance themselves from the village and get into the clear. They had already hurried past *Zmajevac* spring, and had begun to climb up the hillside toward Desolate Hill, when there was increased shooting around Ovčina, and shouting raised from house to house: 'Don't let them get away! They've kidnapped the *Kmet*'s daughter!' The *Zarožani* simply climbed higher. Guns also barked, it could be said, after them.

When they reached the top of Desolate Hill they halted.

Everyone was so out of breath that they were barely able to breathe. Radojka clung to Strahinja, shaking, unable to utter even a word. From below the guns and shouting drew nigh.

-'Come on, people!' said Old Man Mirko. 'There he is with a mob. He could hurt someone.'

-'I don't want to run from him anymore,' said Purko, out of breath. 'Even if it means spilling blood.'

-'Neither do I,' agreed Ćebo.

-'Stop! Thieves!' Živan's voice was heard from below.

-'There they are, Živan! Strike!' someone else was heard and a gun barked.

-'Strahinja, hide that child behind the beech tree!' said Old Man Mirko. 'Those lunatics aren't joking!'

-'Prepare an ambush!' said Purko to the others.

Everyone aimed their guns downward and took cover, some behind a beech, some behind a rock.

Then Živan appeared with his people on the hill and shouted:

-'There they are! Thieves! You'll see who Živan is!'

-'Back off!' bellowed Ćebo from behind a beech. 'Or blood will be spilled!'

-'Is that you Ćebo?' shouted Živan and aimed his gun at the voice.

-'So, is it going to be like that?' Ćebo hollered and fired his pistol.

-'Shoot at the wind, people!'[41] shouted *Kmet* Purko to the

---

[41] An expression meaning to shoot over their heads.

company, 'so we don't injure anyone!'

-'Are you also there, *Kmet*?' shouted Živan, because he heard Purko's voice. 'Halt!' and he let fly at the voice.

-'Don't fire at your *Kum* on St. John's Day!' responded Purko, discharging his pistol by accident.

Guns blazed from one side and the other. Both raised a hue. All that could be heard was:

-'Hold on Purko!'

-'Ha, you're not even a dog!'

-'Over here, people, we're getting killed!'

-'Don't give up, blood is being spilt.'

-'Stop, Živan!'

-'Ooo, you piece of crap, Ćebo!'

-'A dog bit me, ow!'

-'Wrap the towel!'[42]

-'It's not anything!'

-'He got scratched by a thorn!'

-'It's a musket ball!'

-'It's a thorn! T'aint no musket ball!'

Then a commotion arose from down in Zarožje: 'Come on people! Look alive! They're killing our *Kmet*! Don't let them!' Guns barked more frequently from down in the village; the tumult and shouting drew ever nearer.

-'Run people, we'll get killed!' shouted one of Živan's company.

---

[42] Serbian folklore and culture imbue the towel with other ceremonial and ritual functions in addition to drying the body. These include – but are not limited to – rituals surrounding marriage, death, burial, marital status, etc.

And before you could blink an eye, only Živan remained on the hilltop. His people had abandoned him. He remained stationary, then shouted;

-'That's alright, *Kum*, that's alright. I'll find you tomorrow!'

After saying that, he too disappeared.

The *Zarožani* quickly headed down towards the village. They met with their own people. The guests at Purko's house and almost all the people had set out to help their *Kmet* and his people in their time of trouble.

When they found them hale and whole, shouts went up, a commotion, a merriment. All that could be heard was: 'You were great! That's what he deserved! You're really heroes!'

And all that racket went straight to Purko's house. Now the merriment and drinking truly commenced, as at a real wedding feast.

* * *

The sun had long since shone and had already jumped two to three rods.[43] The *Zarožani*, like civilized people, slept a little, then arose and continued their conversations, merriment, and drinking. It was Sunday and no work of any kind awaited them.

Kmet Purko, Old Man Mirko and several other of the most select men had already agreed to go with Strahinja and Radojka to the priest and let him marry them. Purko would be best man,[44] because he was already Godfather to Radojka;[45] the *stari svat*[46] would be Old Man

---

[43] The shadow on the sundial had already moved by two or three rods.
[44] The best man is called '*Kum*.'

Mirko, and the *dever*[47] would be Srdan, he being the youngest among them.

No sooner had they agreed to this, then someone called from above on Desolate Hill:

-'Oh, Purko!'

-'Who's that calling?' asked Purko and looked over there.

-'It's Živan, by God!' said Srdan.

-'And there are some people with him!' added Strahinja.

-'Oh, Purko,' called Živan even louder from above.

-'Yeah, yeah,' answered Purko.

-'Come out, a little over there, come out!'

Purko came out to the gate. Everyone fell silent so they could hear what would happen.

-'Why are you calling? Why?' Purko shouted at Živan.

-'Return my child to me or there will be trouble!' shouted Živan.

-'Turn away from such a fool's errand,' answered Purko. 'Come on and let's make merry, like civilized people.'

-'Hah! There shall be nothing of that while I am alive!'

-'Then go back from whence you came!'

-'Return my child to me or I'll bring my people; then there will be surprises! I'll judge you in front of everyone.'

-'Judge in your own village, but here, never! Here we judge!

---

[45] The Godfather is also called '*Kum.*'

[46] The *stari svat* (old guest) was typically the uncle of the bridegroom assigned to greet guests, raise toasts, and lift the atmosphere of the wedding feast. Often the responsibilities overlapped with those of the best man.

[47] The *Dever* is typically the brother of the bridegroom, assigned to guard the bride before the wedding and to give her away.

We're going to the priest; let him marry them!'

  -'That marriage is worthless, absolutely nothing'

  -'And why not? Why? Isn't our priest any good?'

  -'Your priest is daft!'

  -'Hey! Don't blaspheme our priest!'

  -'Your priest is daft! Daft! He goes and digs up vampires!'

  -'Well, we'll just see if he's daft!' shouted Purko, then turned to his people: 'Let's go to our priest, brothers. Let him stand there and watch as much as he likes. Let's go to the priest right away!'

  -'But with the state he's in, he could raise his village against us!' said Srdan.

  -'What do you mean the village, Srdan? God be with you,' said Purko. 'There'll be nothing of it.'

  -'Let him raise it,' said Ćebo. 'We're not afraid of them!'

Živan continued to shout from up on the hill, threatening, cursing.

But the *Zarožani* didn't heed him. They arose with Strahinja and Radojka and truly went to the priest for a wedding.

* * *

And again the merriment was at Purko's house. All the *Zarožani* descended on the wedding feast. There they could sing, dance, drink, and fire guns. Noon had already long passed. When again, someone called from the top of Desolate Hill:

  -'Oh, Purko! Oh, Purko!'

-'Who's shouting? Hey!' answered Purko and moved a bit forward.

-'It's me! Me!'

-'Well look there! It's Old Man Sredoje!'

-'What's he want?' inquired Ćebo, and everyone hushed to listen.

-'Is Purko there?' Old Man Sredoje shouted again from above.

-'He is, he is,' answered Purko.

-'Ask him on his honor that there won't be a brawl?'

-'Ah hah! He's frightened!' said Old Man Mirko.

-'And he has reason to be,' added Ćebo.

-'If there won't be,' shouted Old Man Sredoje, 'then we'll come as friends.'

-'Is it on your word of honor?' asked Purko.

-'It is! Truly it is!' continued Old Man Sredoje.

-'Then tell Živan to come!' shouted Purko. 'The door is open to him!'

-'What did you say?' asked the old man from above.

-'Come, brother! Freely!' shouted Purko as loudly as he could.

Old Man Sredoje waved his hand towards the other side of the hill. After a short wait, Živan and a dozen men appeared. All proceeded towards Zarožje. The *Zarožani* came far out to meet them.

-'Welcome.'

-'Happy festivities.'

-'We're yours now!'

-'How are you, Ćebo?'

-'Welcome, *Kum*!'

A merry din arose among them.

Guns fired in celebration. Everyone present kissed as though they were friends and good neighbors, and they went in front of Purko's house.

Živan was still pouting a bit, but finally he had no other choice than to make peace with Strahinja, and with Radojka, and with everyone...

And then the merriment began, allegedly such as could not be remembered. For three days all they did was eat and drink, sing and dance... When everyone had satisfied himself, some said that they should probably head home.

Živan and Purko almost got into a fight over Strahinja. Purko tried to get him to remain in Zarožje and accept him into his home and *zadruga*.[48] Živan wouldn't permit it – rather he invited them to Ovčina, where he would receive them into his home and *zadruga*. Finally, Strahinja thanked both Purko and Živan and said that he would like most of all to go to his own home, because, as he said, his own home meant his own freedom.

And so the *Ovčanci* headed home with the groom and the bride. The *Zarožani* escorted them as far as the top of Desolate Hill. There they kissed goodbye and parted as friends. The *Ovčanci* went to Ovčina, singing and firing off their guns, and the *Zarožani* returned to Zarožje, they too singing and firing off guns.

Both villages settled down. The *Zarožani* found a miller; the watermill began to grind day and night. No one ever again

---

[48] A *zadruga* is an extended family collective/cooperative household grouping prevalent in agrarian regions among the South Slavs.

complained that he was hungry and that there wasn't any flour.

They say that for a long time that butterfly continued to kill small children in both Zarožje and Ovčina, and then, even it disappeared.

Even to this day, old men and women speak about Živan Dušman, about Strahinja, about Sava Savanović, and about the Zarožje watermill, and swear on all the wonders of the world that everything happened exactly that way, and that the old people told them thus.

* * *

Printed in the USA
CPSIA information can be obtained
at www.ICGtesting.com
LVHW011558221223
767236LV00004B/330